THE YETI FILES

Attack of the Kraken

KEVIN SHERRY

This one is dedicated to your teachers.
They care about you more than you can imagine.

Library of Congress Cataloging-in-Publication Data

Names: Sherry, Kevin, author, illustrator. I Sherry, Kevin. Yeti files ; 3.
Title: Attack of the kraken / Kevin Sherry.
Description: First edition. I New York : Scholastic Press, 2016. I ©2016 I Series: The Yeti files ; 3 I Summary: The merfolk of Atlantis have called in yeti Blizz Richards and his team of cryptozoologists to capture the kraken that is attacking their city, but when he starts to investigate, Blizz realizes that there is a lot the merfolk are not telling him—and something fishy is definitely going on.
Identifiers: LCCN 2015047306 I ISBN 9780545857819
Subjects: LCSH: Yeti—Juvenile fiction. I Mermen—Juvenile fiction. I Kraken—Juvenile fiction. I Atlantis (Legendary place) —Juvenile fiction. I Conspiracies—Juvenile fiction. I CYAC: Mystery and detective stories. I Yeti—Fiction. I Mermen—Fiction. I Kraken—Fiction. I Atlantis (Legendary place)—Fiction. I Conspiracies—Fiction.
Classification: LCC PZ7.S549 At 2016 I DDC 813.6--dc23
LC record available at http://lccn.loc.gov/2015047306

10 9 8 7 6 5 4 3 2 1   16 17 18 19 20

Printed in the U.S.A. 23
First edition, May 2016

Book design by Carol Ly

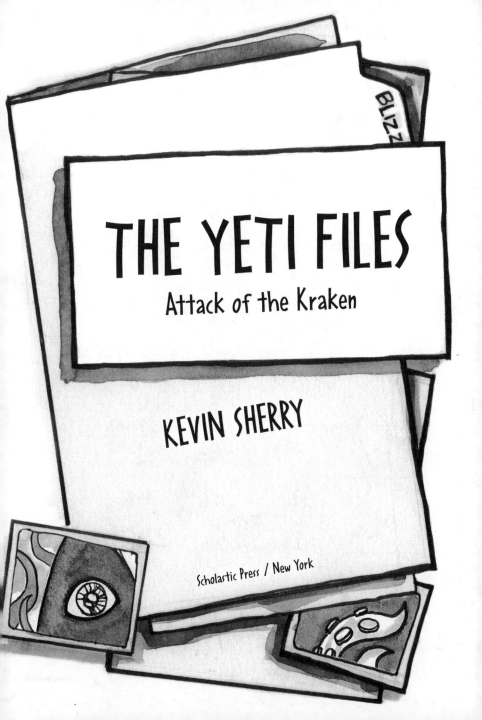

THE YETI FILES

Attack of the Kraken

KEVIN SHERRY

Scholastic Press / New York

Thanks to Mom, Dad, Brian, Teresa Kietlinski, Devlin Rice, Patrick Raube, Valeska Populoh, Michael Lamason, Katherine Fahey, Carlyn Thomas, Matt Gemmel, Ed Schrader, Dan Deacon, Bucketlist, Emily Wexler, Bun Magic Pro Tour, Remington, and Baltimore.

Chapter 1:
A PECULIAR PET

Gunthar! Alex! Come inside.

The Cryptosub is fixed. It's almost time to take it on our next mission!

You see that over there?

That's Alexander and Gunthar's igloo.

They love playing in it. But they always end up arguing.

I say, let goblins and elves be goblins and elves!

I'll just give them a little more time out here.

3

You won't be able to keep it a secret from Blizz forever. And anyway, it's super dangerous.

That thing is a wild animal. You can't tame it.

SQUAWK!

Chapter 2:
TRAVEL BY SUB

···

Hey, guys!

Frank and I got the new and improved
Cryptosub up and running.

SONAR GIZMO

JET THRUSTERS

HIGH-SPEED PROPELLER

ROBOT ARMS

Anyway, if you read
The Yeti Files #2:
Monsters on the Run,
you will remember that we
got an urgent alert from the
merfolk of Atlantis.

CLANK!

SHAMELESS
PLUG

OVER IT.

You may have heard of **mermaids**—

half fish, half ladies. Real merfolk are people who have spent so much time in the water, they have adapted to living in it all of the time.

MERFOLK SWIMMING GEAR

WEBBED GLOVES

SLEEK TAIL

STYLISH FASHION SENSE

Like fish, merfolk have gills so they can breathe underwater. But like people, they can also use their mouths—and their legs! Most merfolk prefer to wear a tail, though. It's just way cooler!

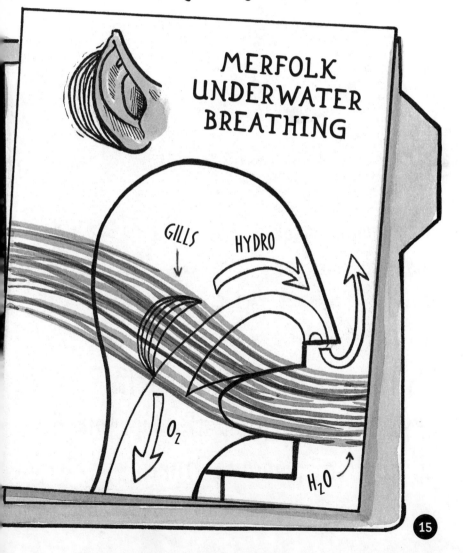

MERFOLK UNDERWATER BREATHING

GILLS

HYDRO

O_2

H_2O

The merfolk live in the lost city of Atlantis.

FLORIDA

BERMUDA

PUERTO RICO

It's an underwater colony somewhere between Florida, Bermuda, and Puerto Rico.

The area is rich with **special crystals** that help the merfolk do all kinds of awesome things.

Crystal technology powers their cities, grows their food, and produces everything they need. It also can make anything disappear, including socks, homework, and human ships that stray into the so-called Bermuda Triangle. We'll travel there to answer their call for help.

To get to Atlantis, we'll go down through the underwater air lock here in my lair.

Its tunnel leads to the Indian Ocean.

UNDERWATER AIR LOCK

INDIAN OCEAN

From there, we travel past Australia (G'day, mate!), swing by Hawaii (Aloha!), and finally arrive at the Bermuda Triangle.

Pack a good book, boys.
It's going to be a long trip!

Chapter 3:
MEET THE MAYOR

....

I hear Atlantis has this great new mayor. He's sending a team to meet us, so we can't be late.

Take a deep breath,
hold on tight, and
don't lose your lunch.

It's go time!

CRYSTAL CRAB SHACK

GIANT SPHERE OF PLATO

POWERFUL WATERFALL

LIGHTHOUSE

AQUA MALL

23

The mayor is right this way.

He's just finishing a meeting with his supporters. They are so proud of how he's helped our city grow.

Atlantis was always a fine city, mind you. But under my leadership it has become truly extraordinary.

I was the first to harness the true power of our **crystals.**

As a young boy,
I studied our crystals carefully.
They power everything in our lives.

Soon I was using them to create **great vehicles** and **industrial machines**. I even perfected a **force field** that shields us from the world above the waves.

BETTER TURN BACK!

ATLANTIS

And now I'm using crystal power to build a **brighter, better Atlantis.**

Which means we must constantly mine the sea for more crystals!

But our whole way of life is being threatened by a **terrible monster!**

SEA TURTLE

BARRACUDA

GIANT SQUID

SQUID

TERRIBLE MONSTER

32

This damage could only have been done by the kraken.

Look at how big the suction marks are!

You must find the kraken and **stop him!**

My trusty security team will help you get started.

You'll need ID, registration, and temporary water insurance. And we'll have to get you all fitted for tails. But first let's go over our Atlantis bylaws:

Law #1: Don't feed the sharks.
Law #2: Never swim alone in a dark alley.
Law #3: Littering the ocean is never allowed.
Law #4: Never interfere with crystal technology.

re crossing a waterway.

Chapter 4:
NEW FRIENDS

I'm glad we snuck outta there.

We have work to do!

CRYSTAL POWER

EXPLORE
EXCEL
EXPAND

He has convinced the merfolk that crystals are the only way to make our lives better.

Crystals have always been important to us.

They power our cities, but they are also the heart of the sea itself. Without them, the ocean and all who live here cannot survive.

But Blacksand only wants them so he can expand the city— and his power over it.

All he cares about is crystals, **crystals,** **crystals!**

And now he's using them to make **bigger machines** to dig out **bigger crystals**.

He is *obsessed!*

41

He has convinced our people with his
impressive technology that
we deserve to own all crystals.

"What do I think of Blacksand? His crystal-powered Internet is the best. My video game screen has never been clearer."

"He has created so many jobs. My son Barnacle is out there driving a forklift . . . and finally off my couch."

"I give his fireworks displays **two thumbs up.** Those crystals can really blow things sky-high!"

"Hasn't anyone noticed that the more the mayor builds, the more the kraken attacks us?"

Oh, Emily Airwalker!

She was a famous pilot and explorer. On a mission many years ago, our crystal power downed her plane.

But the merfolk saved her. She was drawn to our way of life, so she decided to remain in Atlantis to study it.

48

She became interested in the myth of the kraken and hoped to one day see the beast with her own eyes.

And so she went looking for it. She would be gone for months at a time, and then one day she disappeared completely.

ATLANTIS HISTORY

Blacksand blames the kraken.

ATLANTIS TIMES
AIRWALKER MISSING!

While Alexander and Gunthar were arguing—again—Coral was leading Blizz to the Museum of Atlantis.

It's the finest museum in the world.

They have collections of the best pieces of both human and cryptid history, art, and science.

The exhibit about Emily Airwalker has lots of information about her life and her search for the kraken.

Hopefully we'll find something useful.

ANCIENT COLUMN

PIECE OF THE GREAT WALL OF ATLANTIS

ORB OF POSEIDON

MERFOLK MASTERPIECES

Slow down!

FIRST AQUA CAR

Nope!

ALERT!

This changes everything!
The kraken isn't the
monster Blacksand is making
him out to be...

We've got to find the kraken before Blacksand does.

Hopefully the map in Emily's journal will lead us to it!

Chapter 6:
ALEX AND GUNTHAR ARE DOIN' FINE

Meanwhile, Frank was nowhere to be found.

Gunthar, do you feel like someone's watching you?

Only you, buddy!

Meanwhile ...

Frank was making a
new friend—as always.

Dolphins love to explore.

And see old pals.

This guy knows cool tricks.

Hello, there!

70

Told you!

Chapter 7:
A CRABBY HELLO

Blizz and Coral had almost reached the cave Emily had written about.

We passed the trench and turned right at the reef.

We should be getting close...

Chapter 8:
TRUTH IN THE DEEP

ORGANIC KELP FARM

SEA MONKEY HOUSE

It's the kraken!
And look who else ...

SLEEPING POD

MINIONS

BREAKFAST
NOOK

EMILY
AIRWALKER

HEART STONE

My journal!

I lost this long ago. I took these notes on my first journey to Kraken's Kavern. And now my many-legged friend is in trouble. I only wish I could help him stop that awful Blacksand from destroying everything!

You see, the mayor of Atlantis doesn't understand how the magic of the sea really works.

There are many kinds of crystals, with many different powers.

They inspire scientific discovery, art, music, food, love, and friendship.

And the most important crystal of all, the **Heart Stone**, keeps the oceans alive and creates harmony around the world.

The mighty kraken is responsible for protecting it from falling into the wrong hands.

I have always allowed the merfolk to take some of the krystals to power Atlantis and so they may live kalmly and kontentedly.

But Mayor Blacksand has gotten greedy!

He has mined too many **krystals**, and that has weakened the **krust** of our **kavern**.

If he doesn't stop, the **kavern** will **krack**.

I'm scared, Blizz Richards.

If he kontinues to drill and finds the Heart Stone, **all will be lost.**

Who knows what damage he might do with a krystal as powerful as the Heart Stone!

But only to protect the
Heart Stone. We would
much rather help our
fellow kreatures.

Chapter 9:
KAVE IN!

....

See what I mean?

Blacksand kontinues whatever the kost. And now he's destroying the walls of our kavern!

But first ...
where are my
crystals?

They may have tried to
destroy our home, but we
kannot let any kreature die.
Even that kruel madman.

Can you believe
that just
happened?!

I'm not going to say
I told you so. But
I told you that wild
animals are dangerous.

And so Alex and Gunthar escaped the food chain.

I give up! Frank is on his own.

Let's go find Blizz.

Chapter 11:
A NEW ATLANTIS

Back at City Hall, a new council was elected to rule Atlantis.

We, the council, sentence you, Julius Blacksand, to one year of hard labor fixing Kraken's Kavern. And you will spend the full year **without your tail!**

No tail?

This council has decided to replace the old laws with three new ones.

Law #1: Take care of the ocean.

Law #2: Respect all creatures.

Law #3: Listen to your sister!